Presented to

Whitney

From

Uncle Robbie & Aunt Sugar
& Jessica

Date

5/24/94

Dedicated

with love

to

MOM

Learning Can Be Fun

Text by Debbie Butcher Wiersma   Illustrated by Samuel J. Butcher

Baker Books

A Division of Baker Book House Co
Grand Rapids, Michigan 49516

First printing, October 1993
Second printing, February 1994

Published by Baker Books
a division of Baker Book House Company
P.O. Box 6287, Grand Rapids, Michigan 49516-6287

Library of Congress Cataloging-in-Publication Data

Wiersma, Debbie Butcher.
    Learning can be fun / text by Debbie Butcher Wiersma ; illustrated by Samuel J. Butcher.
      p.   cm.
    Summary: Simple text and illustrations featuring Precious Moments characters present the alphabet, numbers from one to ten, shapes, colors, days of the week, months of the year, and various occupations.
    ISBN 0-8010-1059-4
    [1. Alphabet. 2. Counting. 3. Shape. 4. Color. 5. Days. 6. Months. 7. Occupations—Fiction.]
I. Butcher, Samuel J. (Samuel John), 1939–   ill. II. Precious moments. III. Title.
PZ7.W63585Le   1993
[E]—dc20   93-11671

Printed in the United States of America

Dear Parents,

I believe, as the title of this book says, that learning **can** be fun. When I was a young girl, my mother would spend hours reading to me and my six brothers and sisters. We didn't realize we were learning things from the pages of those books. We were just having fun!

When my father would let me mix his paints or show me how to blend colors, I didn't know that I was learning the basics of art that I would one day pass on to my children. I was having too much fun!

While writing this book (with a little help from big brother Jon), I've tried to bring back the magical innocence of childhood. I've tried to make **Learning Can Be Fun** not only a book that children will enjoy but one that will make parents smile, too.

Take time to talk with your child about the things you read here. You'll be building some very precious memories.

Thank you,

Debbie Butcher Wiersma

Contents

A is for **A**ngel
way up in the sky.

B is for **B**aby
and a **B**right **B**utterfly.

C is for Clumsy Clown
falling on the ground.

D is for Donnie's Dog
and the shiny
Dime he found.

E is for Elephant
giving a mouse a shower.

F is For some Friendly Frogs
sitting by a Flower.

G is for Greedy Goat
Getting very fat.

H is for **H**appy **H**enry
in **H**is cowboy **H**at.

I is for **I**ce cream
on a sunny day.

J is for baby Jesus
sleeping in the hay.

K is for Kitten
so cuddly and nice.

L is for Lemonade
and Licking Lots of ice.

M is for Milking
and two Merry Mice.

N is for Naughty
and Not being Nice.

O is for **O**wls
sitting in a tree.

P is for **P**apoose
wrapped so tenderly.

Q is for a Queen bee
chasing off a bear.

R is for Rhinosaurus
who doesn't have much hair.

S is for Sodas
and Sharing a Sip.

T is for **T**urtle
who's **T**aking a **T**rip.

U is for **U**nicorn
dancing on a cloud.

V is for the **V**iolin
that **V**ictor plays too loud.

W is for **W**edding,
a happy groom and bride.

X is for **X**-ray
to show what's inside.

Y is for Yak
and a Yummy snack.

Z is for **Z**ebra
all striped white and black.

Let's Look Again!

A a   B b   C c   D d

E e   F f   G g   H h

I i   J j   K k   L l   M m

N n   O o   P p   Q q

R r   S s   T t   U u   V v

W w   X x   Y y   Z z

One to Ten And Back Again!

ONE Bouncing Ball

TWO Pretty Parrots

THREE Bright Balloons

FOUR Fun Flowers

FIVE Big Bows

SIX Buzzing Bees

SEVEN Happy Hearts

EIGHT Shining Stars

NINE Sparkling Snowflakes

TEN Beautiful Butterflies

Let's Look Again

10 Ten Beautiful Butterflies

9 Nine Sparkling Snowflakes

8 Eight Shining Stars

7 Seven Happy Hearts

6 Six Buzzing Bees

5 Five Big Bows

4 Four Fun Flowers

3 Three Bright Balloons

2 Two Pretty Parrots

1 One Big Ball

One
+
one
=
FUN!

Let's play a game
That's lots of fun
The number we'll start with
Is number . . .

ONE!

We'll start with one foot
That has one shoe
If I give you another
you'll have . . .

2

TWO!

If you have four apples
And you give one to me
The number of apples
You'll have is . . .

3

THREE!

If you have three cookies
And I give you one more
The number of cookies
You have is . . .

FOUR!

If you have four bees
In a buzzing bee hive
And I give you one more
Then you'll have . . .

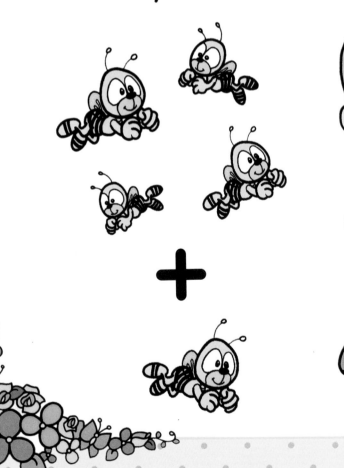

5

FIVE!

If you have five puppies
That play with five sticks
And I give you another
Then you'll have . . .

+

SIX!

If you see six stars
Twinkling in heaven
And one more appears
Then there are . . .

SEVEN!

If seven friends
Are learning to skate
And one more joins in
Then there are . . .

EIGHT!

If you have eight blocks
And I give you mine
The number of blocks
You have will be . . .

NINE!

If you have nine pigs
In a little pig pen
And I give you one more
Then you will have . . .

+

10
TEN!

Now that we've gone
from one to ten
you can go back
and do it again!

Let's Look Again!

$$\text{👟} + \text{👟} = 2$$

$$\text{🍎🍎🍎🍎} - \text{🍎} = 3$$

$$\text{🍪🍪🍪} + \text{🍪} = 4$$

$$\text{🐜🐜🐜🐜} + \text{🐜} = 5$$

$$\text{////} + \text{/} = 6$$

$$\text{★★★★★★} + \text{★} = 7$$

$$+ = 8$$

$$+ = 9$$

$$+ = 10$$

Monday's child . . .

is fair of face.

Tuesday's child . . .

is full of grace.

Wednesday's child . . .

is full of woe.

Thursday's child . . .

has far to go.

Friday's child . . .

is loving and giving.

Saturday's child . . .

works hard for a living.

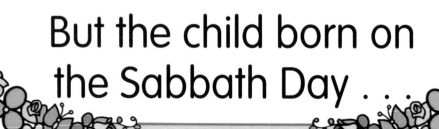

But the child born on
the Sabbath Day . . .

is happy and sweet
and loves to play.

Let's Look Again!

Monday

Tuesday

Wednesday

Thursday

Friday

Saturday

The Sabbath Day . . .
Sunday

January starts the year
with tiny flakes of snow

Falling softly through the clouds
to children down below.

February sends its love
in one big Valentine.

This angel made a special card.
It says, "Will you be mine?"

March is full of windy days
when robins come to sing.

The birds return from far away
promising the spring.

April's busy pouring rain
on all the springtime flowers.

Children come outside to play,
enjoying springtime showers!

In **May** the buds are blossoming
with flowers everywhere.

All the colors of the rainbow
dancing in the air.

June is a month of starry nights.
The days are warm and clear.

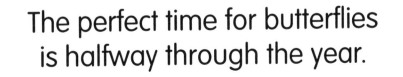

The perfect time for butterflies
is halfway through the year.

July brings nights to sit outside
and look up at the sky.

We say, "I'm proud of where I live,"
and watch the fireworks fly.

August is a lazy month.
The moon has sleepy eyes.

A million little lights from heaven
Twinkle in the midnight skies.

September school bells ring
again. The buses run once more.

Oh, no! a worm found teacher's apple,
He ate it all except the core!

October fills our days with gold
and air so crisp and clean.

Children are laughing as they play,
in the brightest leaves you've ever seen.

November is a month to think
of all the things you love:

your family, and Thanksgiving,
and your Father up above.

December brings us Christmas Day
when God sent down his Son.

It's a day of love and joy
and fun for everyone.

Let's Look Again

January

February

March

April

May

June

July

August

September

October

November

December

What Shape Am I?

Triangle

A triangle has three straight sides and three pointed angles.

Can you find these triangles on the next page?

Circle

A circle is round like a wheel. Every point on its curve is the same distance from its center.

Can you find these circles on the next page?

Oval

An oval is like a stretched-out circle. It is shaped like an egg.

Can you find these ovals on the next page?

Square

A square is shaped like a box.
It has four equal sides
and four corners.

Can you find these squares on the next page?

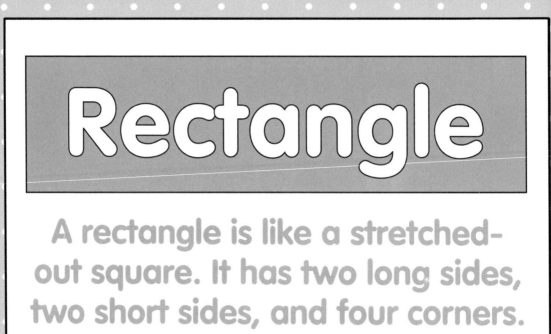

Rectangle

A rectangle is like a stretched-out square. It has two long sides, two short sides, and four corners.

Can you find these rectangles on the next page?

Let's Look Again!

Square

Circle

Triangle

Oval

Rectangle

Orange Is The

Color Of Half A

GiraffE!

Orange is the color of half a giraffe and the fruit that his monkey friend eats.

Purple is the color of little round grapes,
the jungle king's most favorite treats.

Green is the color of parrots and snakes and a jungle full of trees.

Yellow is the color of ripe bananas
and honey and bumblebees.

Red is a ladybug eating a leaf and berries so tender and sweet.

Blue are the flowers and ripe berry fruits
the elephant loves to eat.

Pink is the color of Debbie's nightgown
and her bunny's a pretty pink, too.

The summertime skies, the pond
down below, and Patti's
new dress are light blue.

Lavender flowers and sweet butterflies make our days pretty and bright.

The clouds in the sky and the daisy
Jon picked
are such a beautiful **white**.

Mint green is for froggies and chocolate mints, balloons and some sweet candy sticks.

Peach is the color of Kerri's new clown who does the most wonderful tricks!

Let's Look Again

Orange

Purple

Yellow

Green

Red

Blue

Pink

Light Blue

Lavender

White

Mint Green

Peach

178

BAKER

My name is Sue and I am a **BAKER**. I make pretty cakes for birthdays and other special times. I use many different colors of frosting to make fancy flowers and designs. My job is fun because I always get to lick the spoon.

WAITER

My name is Michael and I am a **WAITER**. It's my job to bring your food to you. It takes a lot of practice to balance my tray full of food. I practice every day, so someday I'll be a very good waiter.

GARDENER

My name is Sara and I'm a **GARDENER**. I love to plant tiny seeds and watch plants grow big and strong. People like the pretty things I grow. It makes me happy to see how my flowers can brighten someone's day.

PHOTOGRAPHER

My name is Colin and I am a **PHOTOGRA-PHER**. My job is very special because I help everyone remember happy times. After I take pictures, I give them to people to put in their photo albums. I love making people smile when I take their pictures.

MUSICIAN

My name is Patti and I'm a **MUSICIAN**. I love to play happy music because it makes me feel so good inside. Music can make other people feel good inside, too. My kitty likes to sit with me and listen to her favorite songs.

POLICEMAN

My name is Cody and I am a **POLICEMAN**. It's my job to make sure everybody is safe. I watch for people who might need help. I also watch for people who forget to follow the rules. Lindsey was riding her tricycle too fast and that could be dangerous. She might not be able to stop in time if somebody got in her way, so I had to give her a ticket to remind her to slow down.

TEACHER

My name is Abby and I am a **TEACHER**. I go to school to learn all of the wonderful things that I will teach. I will help children learn to read and I will show them how to add numbers together. I practice with my little brother and it makes both of us so happy when he learns new things.

PAINTERS

Our names are Jenny and Jonnie and we're **PAINTERS**. We paint houses for people and animals. Everything looks so pretty and new with a nice coat of paint. Sometimes we disagree about which colors to use, but Tippy doesn't mind.

CHEF

My name is Philip and I am a **CHEF**. I cook delicious dinners for people. Chefs have to go to cooking school to learn all of those wonderful recipes, but for now my puppy and I practice with mud pies!

SECRETARY

My name is Gerri and I am a **SECRETARY**. This is a very busy job because everybody depends on me to get things done. I pay the bills, type letters, and answer the telephone all day long. Sometimes I get tired from doing all this hard work, but it makes me happy to know how helpful I'm being.

BARBER

My name is Joe and I am a **BARBER**. It's my job to cut hair. I am very careful with my scissors and comb, so you will look just right. Barbers go to school to learn how to cut hair, but for now I just practice with my little sister. Doesn't she look beautiful?

NURSE

My name is Becky and I am a **NURSE**. My job is very important because I have to make sure everyone gets the right medicine. Sometimes I have to give Teddy a shot. That makes me sad because I know shots hurt for a few seconds. I always kiss him all better. The medicine I give Teddy will make him well and that will make us both happy.

DENTIST

My name is Justin and I am a **DENTIST**. I teach children how to brush their teeth every day so they won't get cavities. I helped my brother get his loose tooth out so his new tooth will have room to grow.

SINGER

My name is Missy and I'm a **SINGER**. I like to practice singing every day so my voice will be strong. When I'm home I hum my favorite songs while I'm playing. Sometimes I sing along with my tape recorder. I dream of being a famous singer someday; but, if I'm not, that's okay, too. Mostly I just like to sing to make myself happy.

PILOT

My name is Dougie and I am a **PILOT**. I love my job because I fly high above the clouds. Being a pilot is hard work and there is a lot to learn, but it's a fun job, too. A pilot can take children to visit their grandparents, and he takes people all around the world to visit beautiful places.

WAITRESS

My name is Stephanie and I'm a **WAITRESS**. It's my job to take your order at a restaurant and serve your food. I like my job because I meet so many people. I'm always nice to the people who sit at my tables because that will help them to have a happy day.

DOCTOR

My name is Matthew and I am a **DOCTOR**. I listen to heartbeats and take temperatures. If you have a sore spot I can patch it up. Children come to see me even when they're not sick so I can make sure they are growing strong and tall.

MOMMY

My name is Kathie and I want to be a
MOMMY someday. I think this is the most
important job that any girl can have. It will
be my job to make sure my children are
safe and warm and loved a lot. I will teach
my children how to be good people. I will
make rules for them to follow so they will be
safe and happy. And sometimes, if they
don't like my rules, I will tell them why rules
are so important. Mommies don't get paid
but they get something even better. They
get lots of hugs and kisses and love from
their children.

DADDY

My name is Sammy and I want to be a **DADDY** someday. It will be my job to take care of my children and love them. I will teach my children many important things and how to be kind and loving to others. This will help them grow up to be caring people. I will make rules for my children to follow, so they will be safe and happy. I think this is the most important job that any boy could have.

Let's Look Again

Baker

Waiter

Gardener

Photographer

Musician

Policeman

Teacher

Painter

Chef

Secretary

Barber

Nurse

Dentist

Singer

Pilot

Waitress

Doctor

Mommy

Daddy

What Have You Learned?

You Can Practice

Name __Whitney__   Date __We three__

Writing the Letters

Name **Whitney** Date **November**

You Can Practice

Name: Whitney   Date: November

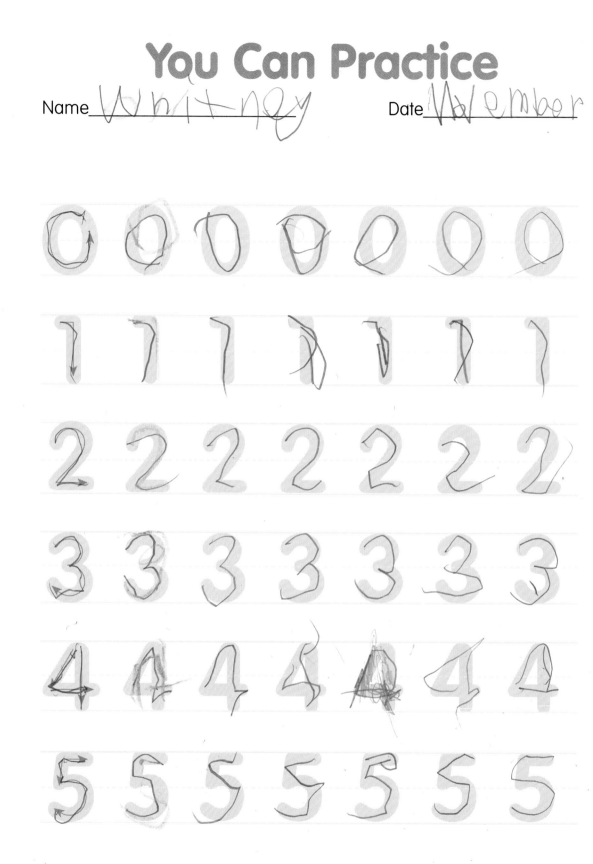

222

Writing the Numbers

Name _Whitney_ Date _November_

You Can Practice

Name ___Whitney___ Date ___November___

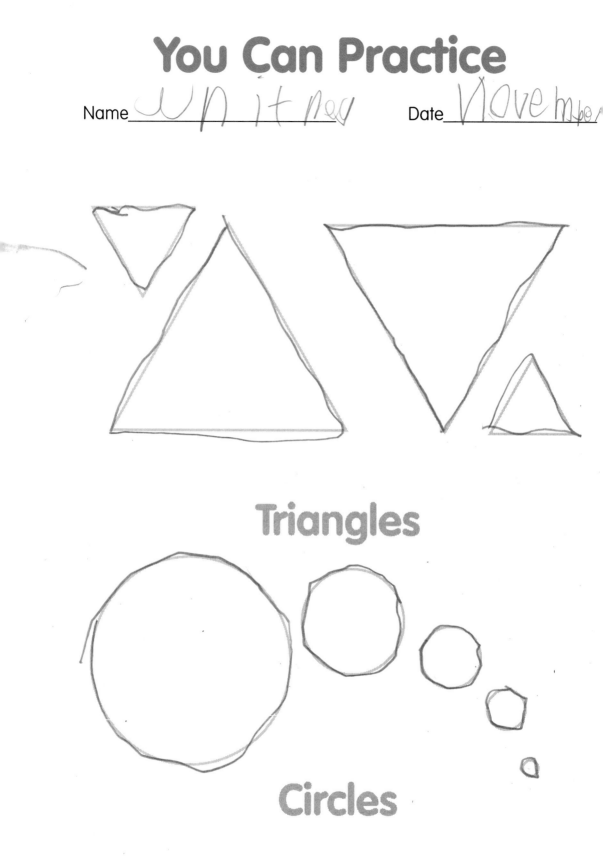

Triangles

Circles

Drawing the Shapes

Name Whitney   Date November

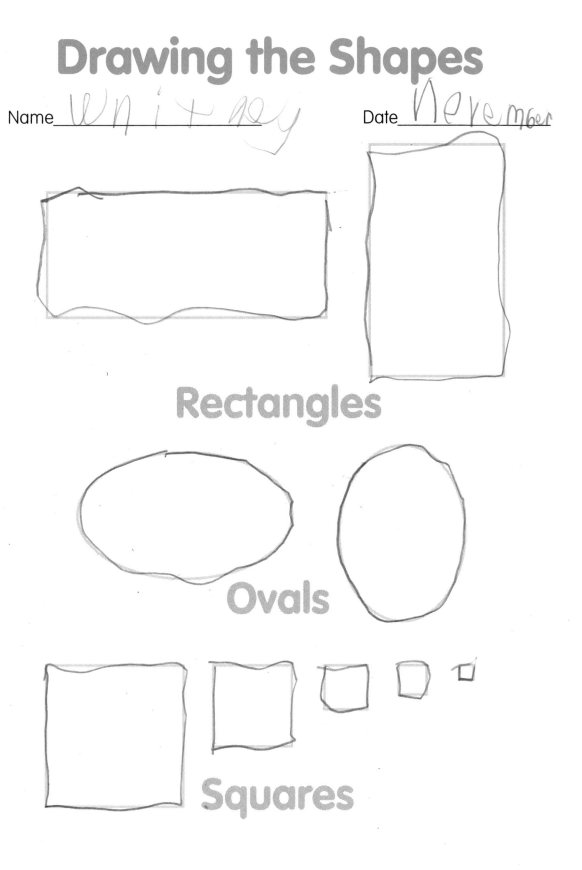

Rectangles

Ovals

Squares

You Can Practice

Name **Whitney**   Date **November**

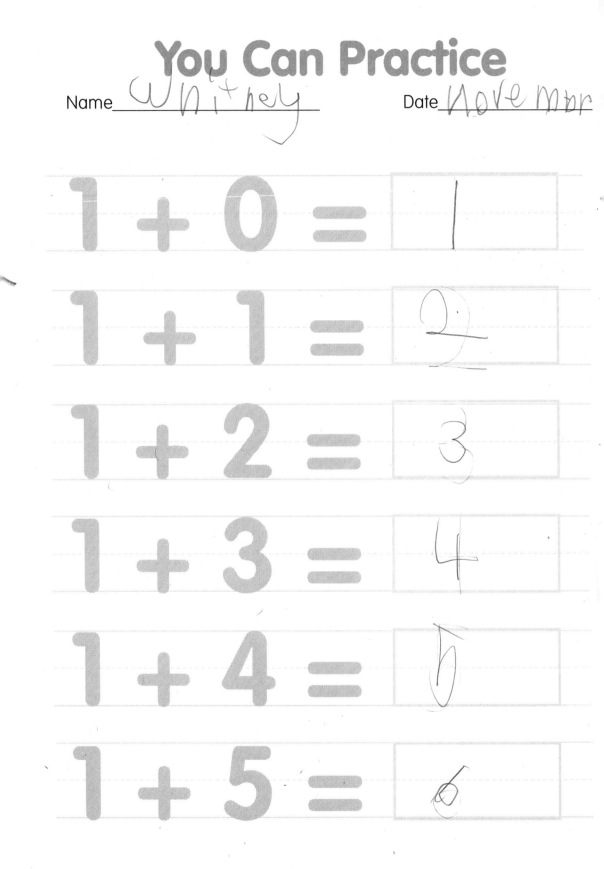

1 + 0 = | 1

1 + 1 = | 2

1 + 2 = | 3

1 + 3 = | 4

1 + 4 = | 5

1 + 5 = | 6

Adding the Numbers

1 + 6 =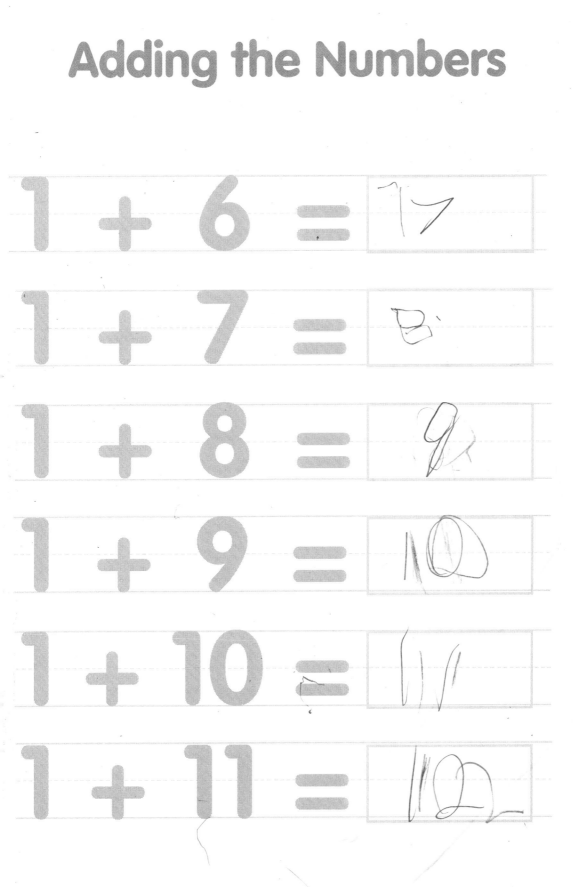

1 + 7 =

1 + 8 =

1 + 9 =

1 + 10 =

1 + 11 =

You Can Practice

Name _Whitney_   Date_____

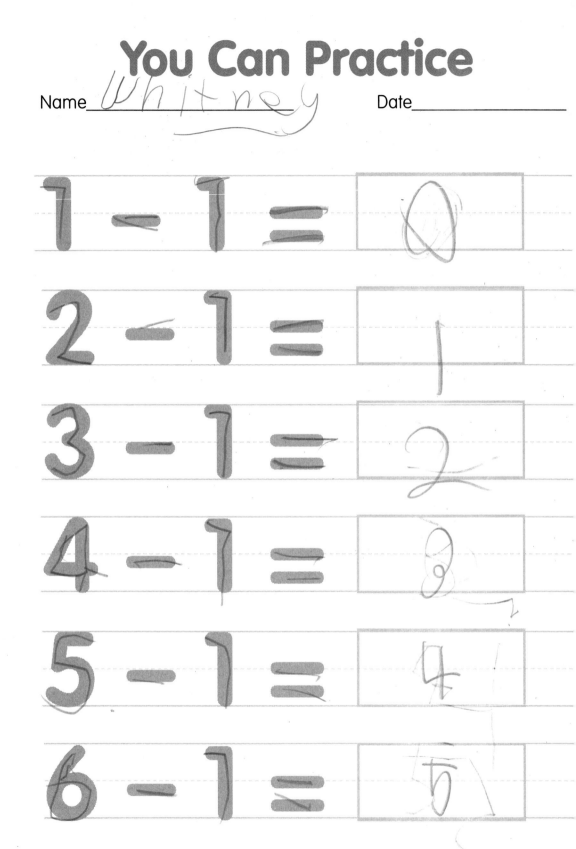

1 − 1 = ☐ 0

2 − 1 = ☐ 1

3 − 1 = ☐ 2

4 − 1 = ☐ 3

5 − 1 = ☐ 4

6 − 1 = ☐ 5

Subtracting the Numbers

Name_____   Date_____

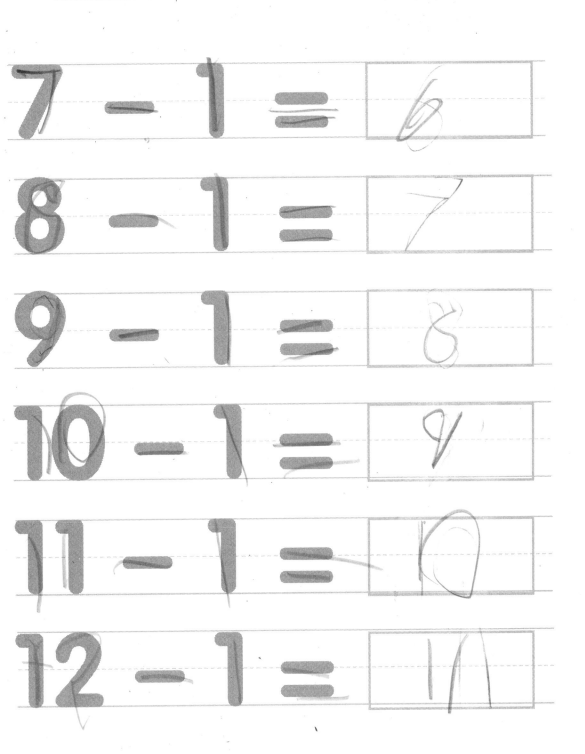

7 − 1 = ☐ 6

8 − 1 = ☐ 7

9 − 1 = ☐ 8

10 − 1 = ☐ 9

11 − 1 = ☐ 10

12 − 1 = ☐ 11

You Can Find the Colors

Purple

You Can Find the Colors

Red

You Can Find the Colors

Blue

You Can Find the Colors

Green

Yellow

You Can Practice

Name_____ Date_____

January

February

March

April

May

June

Writing the Months

Name_____   Date_____

July

August

September

October

November

December

You Can Practice

Name_____   Date_____

Monday

Tuesday

Wednesday

Thursday

Writing the Days

Name_____ Date_____

Friday

Saturday

Sunday